THIS JOURNAL BELONGS TO:

Eliana

Harry Potter™

WISDOM

A GUIDED JOURNAL FOR
EMBRACING YOUR INNER

RAVENCLAW™

INSIGHT
EDITIONS

San Rafael • Los Angeles • London

INTRODUCTION

WISE. WITTY. CREATIVE. These are the traits of Ravenclaw house, the cleverest house at Hogwarts, draped in its graceful colors of blue and silver and represented by a raven. There are many notable and beloved Ravenclaw characters in the Harry Potter films. From Luna Lovegood and Cho Chang to renowned wandmaker Mr. Ollivander, Ravenclaws are represented by a wide range of witches and wizards. But what does it mean to truly be a Ravenclaw? How can you bring out your innate qualities of wisdom, wit, and creativity and apply them to your everyday life?

This journal, composed of 52 weeks of prompts, will help you reflect on, connect with, and develop the Ravenclaw inside you. Each week includes two kinds of prompts. The first is a simple form where you can record daily acts of wisdom, wit, or creativity. Taking the structure of a simple "one-line-a-day" journal, this form allows you to record small "Ravenclaw moments" that you encounter throughout your week. There is no pressure to fill one out every day. After all, you may not have the opportunity to excercise your wisdom every day. But it gives you an opportunity to notice and note small ways that you embody your Ravenclaw persona. The second prompt goes deeper, referencing specific quotes, moments, places, or characters from the films and inviting you to think about how being a Ravenclaw shapes and affects your life. These prompts include freewriting, letter writing, list making, coloring, and more.

The Harry Potter films have inspired us, now it's time to explore further and embrace your inner Ravenclaw.

WEEK 1

RAVENCLAW MOMENTS:

Daily Acts of Wisdom, Wit, and Creativity

Monday

Tuesday

Wednesday

Thursday

I was salting the chips and
I said: "Oh mam, these chips are
just like you, mam."
Wit

Friday

Saturday

Sunday

WEEK 1

RAVENCLAWS, LIKE LUNA LOVEGOOD, CHO CHANG,
and Professor Flitwick, rely on their wisdom, wit, and creativity to
accomplish their goals. By purposefully embracing your inner Ravenclaw
qualities, you are taking active steps to realize your dreams. What are you
hoping to achieve or discover by using this journal? How do you see your
Ravenclaw qualities helping you do this?

I wish to gain wisdom
wit, and creativity with this boo

WEEK 2

RAVENCLAW MOMENTS:
Daily Acts of Wisdom, Wit, and Creativity

Monday

Tuesday

Wednesday

Thursday

Friday

Saturday

Sunday

WEEK 2

COLORING MEDITATIONS

The Sorting Hat sorts each Hogwarts student into their house on their first night at school, taking into account their background, talents, personalities, and personal choice. Due to your wisdom, wit, and creativity, you have been sorted into Ravenclaw. Color in the hat below, and decorate the rest of the page with iconography and embellishments that represent your identity as a Ravenclaw.

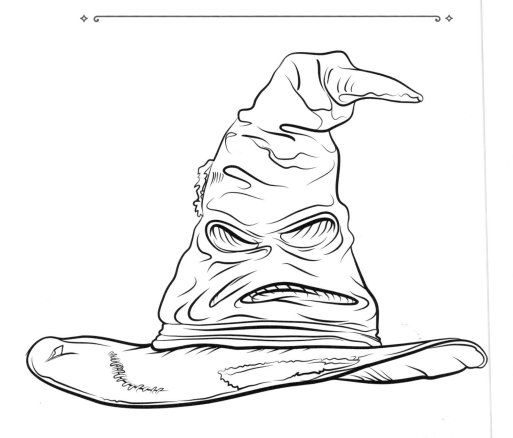

WEEK 3

RAVENCLAW MOMENTS:
Daily Acts of Wisdom, Wit, and Creativity

Monday

Tuesday

Wednesday

Thursday

Friday

Saturday

Sunday

WEEK 3

IN *HARRY POTTER AND THE SORCERER'S STONE,* Harry discovers the Mirror of Erised in an unused classroom at Hogwarts. When he looks into it, he sees his parents. As Professor Dumbledore later explains, the mirror shows the viewer whatever their heart most desires. What do you think you would see if you looked in the mirror? Do you see a connection to your identity as a Ravenclaw? What is it?

I see myself, I've lost the fudge I have, and I've found who I will be when I'm grown.

WEEK 4

RAVENCLAW MOMENTS:
Daily Acts of Wisdom, Wit, and Creativity

Monday

Tuesday

Wednesday

Thursday

Friday

Saturday

Sunday

WEEK 4

THERE ARE MANY AMAZING Ravenclaw characters in the Harry Potter films. Who is your favorite? In what way do you think this character embodies the traits of the house?

WEEK 5

RAVENCLAW MOMENTS:

Daily Acts of Wisdom, Wit, and Creativity

Monday

_____

_____

_____

_____

_____

Tuesday

_____

_____

_____

_____

_____

Wednesday

_____

_____

_____

_____

_____

Thursday

Friday

Saturday

Sunday

WEEK 5

"Your triumphs will earn you points. Any rule-breaking and you will lose points."

—Professor McGonagall, *Harry Potter and the Sorcerer's Stone*

It's important to celebrate our victories.
Make a list of five recent accomplishments you achieved that
you believe would earn you points for Ravenclaw. Award yourself
with the number of points you think you earned. Good job!

1. _____

_____

_____

_____ *Points:* _____

2. _____

_____

_____

_____ *Points:* _____

3. _____

_____

_____

_____ *Points:* _____

4. _____

_____

_____

_____ *Points:* _____

5. _____

_____

_____

_____ *Points:* _____

WEEK 6

RAVENCLAW MOMENTS:

Daily Acts of Wisdom, Wit, and Creativity

Monday

Tuesday

Wednesday

Thursday

Friday

Saturday

Sunday

WEEK 6

ON HARRY'S FIRST DAY AT HOGWARTS, he and Ron
get lost and are late to class. As a Ravenclaw, imagine how you
would spend your first day at Hogwarts.

WEEK 7

Monday

Tuesday

Wednesday

Thursday

Friday

Saturday

Sunday

WEEK 7

OUR SKILLS AND TALENTS OFTEN reflect the inner qualities we naturally possess. For example, Harry is a skilled flier, a talent that could be said to reflect the Gryffindor traits of daringness and nerve. What specific skills and talents do you possess, and how do you feel they relate to your qualities as a Ravenclaw?

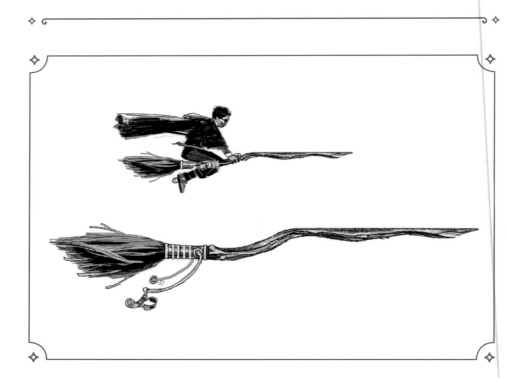

ABOVE: Concept art of Harry and the Firebolt by Dermot Power.

THIS PAGE: Concept art by Adam Brockbank.

WEEK 8

RAVENCLAW MOMENTS:

Daily Acts of Wisdom, Wit, and Creativity

Monday

Tuesday

Wednesday

Thursday

Friday

Saturday

Sunday

WEEK 8

PROFESSOR FLITWICK is the head of Ravenclaw house during Harry's time at Hogwarts. There is no question that teachers, particularly those we work closely with, have a huge effect on the kind of person we grow up to be. Write a letter to your "head of house"—a teacher or mentor who helped you develop your Ravenclaw qualities—reflecting on what they taught you and thanking them for being part of your journey.

WEEK 9

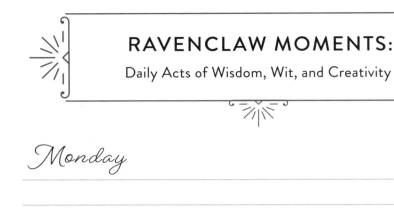

RAVENCLAW MOMENTS:
Daily Acts of Wisdom, Wit, and Creativity

Monday

Tuesday

Wednesday

Thursday

Friday

Saturday

Sunday

WEEK 9

Aside from being the head of Ravenclaw house, Professor Flitwick is also the Charms teacher at Hogwarts. In one memorable *Harry Potter and the Sorcerer's Stone* scene, he teaches the first-years *Wingardium Leviosa*—the Levitation Charm. How do you think Professor Flitwick's qualities as a Ravenclaw are represented in his personality as a teacher? What do you think you could learn from him, both as a Ravenclaw and as a person?

WEEK 10

RAVENCLAW MOMENTS:
Daily Acts of Wisdom, Wit, and Creativity

Monday

_____
_____
_____
_____

Tuesday

_____
_____
_____
_____

Wednesday

_____
_____
_____
_____

Thursday

Friday

Saturday

Sunday

WEEK 10

"We've all got both light and dark inside us. What matters is the part we choose to act on. That's who we really are."

—Sirius Black, *Harry Potter and the Order of the Phoenix*

Sirius Black speaks this powerful quote to Harry in *Harry Potter and the Order of the Phoenix* at a moment when Harry is feeling scared, anxious, and insecure in his identity. This quote could be interpreted to mean that we all have our strong points and our weak points, our positive attributes and our flaws. Ravenclaws are usually described as wise, witty, and creative. But they occasionally also have a reputation for being stuck-up. Think about two moments in your life, one when your behavior reflected the "light" side of Ravenclaw and one when it reflected the "dark" side. Describe these events on the next page. What can you learn from them?

Light:

_____

_____

_____

_____

_____

_____

_____

_____

_____

Dark:

_____

_____

_____

_____

_____

_____

_____

_____

_____

WEEK 11

RAVENCLAW MOMENTS:
Daily Acts of Wisdom, Wit, and Creativity

Monday

Tuesday

Wednesday

Thursday

Friday

Saturday

Sunday

WEEK 11

IN *HARRY POTTER AND THE ORDER OF THE PHOENIX*, Harry meets Luna Lovegood, an open-minded, clever, and quirky witch who doesn't let other people's opinions get in the way of achieving her goals. Write down three long-term goals you are currently working on. How do you see your assets as a Ravenclaw helping you accomplish these aspirations?

1. _____

_____

_____

_____

2. _____

_____

_____

_____

3. _____

_____

_____

_____

WEEK 12

RAVENCLAW MOMENTS:

Daily Acts of Wisdom, Wit, and Creativity

Monday

Tuesday

Wednesday

Thursday

Friday

Saturday

Sunday

WEEK 12

"Happiness can be found, even in the darkest of times, if one only remembers to turn on the light."

—Professor Dumbledore, *Harry Potter and the Prisoner of Azkaban*

List ten things that bring joy to your Ravenclaw heart.
Refer back to these when you are experiencing times of trouble or stress.

1. _____

2. _____

3. _____

4. _____

5. _____

_____

_____

6. _____

_____

_____

7. _____

_____

_____

8. _____

_____

_____

9. _____

_____

_____

10. _____

_____

_____

WEEK 13

RAVENCLAW MOMENTS:
Daily Acts of Wisdom, Wit, and Creativity

Monday

_____

_____

_____

_____

_____

Tuesday

_____

_____

_____

_____

_____

Wednesday

_____

_____

_____

_____

_____

Thursday

Friday

Saturday

Sunday

WEEK 13

IN *HARRY POTTER AND THE DEATHLY HALLOWS – PART 1,*
Xenophilius Lovegood sells Harry and his friends out to the Death Eaters
when they arrive at his house seeking information about the Deathly
Hallows. He later tearfully explains that the Death Eaters have captured
Luna and are holding her as punishment for Xenophilius's support of
Harry in *The Quibbler*. Do you think Xenophilius made the right, or at
least the understandable, choice in that moment? Knowing what he knew
at the time, would you have made the same choice? Why or why not?

WEEK 14

RAVENCLAW MOMENTS:
Daily Acts of Wisdom, Wit, and Creativity

Monday

Tuesday

Wednesday

Thursday

Friday

Saturday

Sunday

WEEK 14

COLORING MEDITATIONS

It's time to show some house pride. Color the Ravenclaw
crest below, and decorate the rest of the page with embellishments
and decorations of your choosing.

WEEK 15

RAVENCLAW MOMENTS:
Daily Acts of Wisdom, Wit, and Creativity

Monday

_____

_____

_____

_____

Tuesday

_____

_____

_____

_____

Wednesday

_____

_____

_____

_____

Thursday

Friday

Saturday

Sunday

WEEK 15

IN THE HARRY POTTER FILMS, Harry Potter and Draco
Malfoy are bitter rivals. Have you ever had a rivalry with another person?
Were they in the same house as you or a different one? What about this
person clashed with your traits as a Ravenclaw?

WEEK 16

RAVENCLAW MOMENTS:
Daily Acts of Wisdom, Wit, and Creativity

Monday

Tuesday

Wednesday

Thursday

Friday

Saturday

Sunday

WEEK 16

HOGWARTS CASTLE IS A MASSIVE, ancient building filled with classrooms, student living spaces, soaring bridges, deep dungeons, high towers, moving staircases, and more than one secret room. Which aspect of the castle would you be most eager to explore? Do you see a connection between this choice and your identity as a Ravenclaw? How so?

THIS PAGE: Concept art of the exterior and interior of Hogwarts castle by Andrew Williamson.

CLOCKWISE FROM TOP LEFT: The exterior of Hogwarts castle by Andrew Williamson; a concept piece of the stained glass window in the prefects' bathroom by Adam Brockbank; a study of the Owlery by Andrew Williamson; a concept sketch of the second-years in Greenhouse Three by Andrew Williamson.

WEEK 17

RAVENCLAW MOMENTS:
Daily Acts of Wisdom, Wit, and Creativity

Monday

Tuesday

Wednesday

Thursday

Friday

Saturday

Sunday

WEEK 17

IMAGINE YOU HAVE THE OPPORTUNITY to interview one
Ravenclaw from the Harry Potter films. Who would you choose?
Write ten questions you would ask them.

10 QUESTIONS FOR: _____

1. _____

_____

_____

2. _____

_____

_____

3. _____

_____

_____

4. _____

_____

_____

5. _____

_____

_____

6. _____

_____

_____

7. _____

_____

_____

8. _____

_____

_____

9. _____

_____

_____

10. _____

_____

_____

WEEK 18

RAVENCLAW MOMENTS:
Daily Acts of Wisdom, Wit, and Creativity

Monday

_____

_____

_____

_____

_____

Tuesday

_____

_____

_____

_____

_____

Wednesday

_____

_____

_____

_____

_____

Thursday

Friday

Saturday

Sunday

WEEK 18

IN *HARRY POTTER AND THE CHAMBER OF SECRETS*, Gilderoy Lockhart comes to Hogwarts as the new Defense Against the Dark Arts teacher. Though he has a reputation as a great wizard (bolstered by his books), it is eventually revealed that he is in fact a liar who's been taking credit for other people's actions. Despite being a Ravenclaw, his only real talent is Memory Charms, which he uses to wipe his victim's memories—hardly an appropriate action for a Ravenclaw. Have you ever acted in a way that went against your house's traits? Why? Describe the circumstances below.

WEEK 19

RAVENCLAW MOMENTS:
Daily Acts of Wisdom, Wit, and Creativity

Monday

Tuesday

Wednesday

Thursday

Friday

Saturday

Sunday

WEEK 19

IN THE HARRY POTTER FILMS, family members are often—but not always—placed in the same houses. While all of the Weasleys are in Gryffindor and all of the Malfoys are in Slytherin, characters like Sirius Black and Parvati and Padma Patil are placed in different houses than other members of their family. What houses would your parents and siblings belong to and why? How do you think this might have contributed to your being a Ravenclaw?

WEEK 20

RAVENCLAW MOMENTS:
Daily Acts of Wisdom, Wit, and Creativity

Monday

Tuesday

Wednesday

Thursday

Friday

Saturday

Sunday

WEEK 20

"*Words are, in my not-so-humble opinion, our most inexhaustible source of magic. Capable of both inflicting injury and remedying it.*"

—Professor Dumbledore, *Harry Potter and the Deathly Hallows - Part 2*

WORDS MATTER!

Write a mantra to help you tap into your inner Ravenclaw.
Use the space below to sketch out your thoughts, and write the final version in the shield on the next page.

MY RAVENCLAW MANTRA

WEEK 21

RAVENCLAW MOMENTS:
Daily Acts of Wisdom, Wit, and Creativity

Monday

Tuesday

Wednesday

Thursday

Friday

Saturday

Sunday

WEEK 21

"Welcome to Hogwarts. Now in a few moments, you will pass through the doors and join your classmates, but before you can take your seats, you must be sorted into your houses. They are Gryffindor, Hufflepuff, Ravenclaw, and Slytherin. Now while you're here, your house will be like your family."

—Professor McGonagall, *Harry Potter and the Sorcerer's Stone*

Think about your closest friends.
What houses do they belong to? Are they the same as you?
How does this affect your relationships?

WEEK 22

RAVENCLAW MOMENTS:
Daily Acts of Wisdom, Wit, and Creativity

Monday

_____

_____

_____

_____

Tuesday

_____

_____

_____

_____

Wednesday

_____

_____

_____

_____

Thursday

Friday

Saturday

Sunday

WEEK 22

THINK ABOUT YOUR OWN SOCIAL INTERACTIONS
as a "typical" Ravenclaw. Write about a time you and your friends
acted like Ravenclaws. What did you do? Why is this particular
memory valuable to you?

WEEK 23

RAVENCLAW MOMENTS:
Daily Acts of Wisdom, Wit, and Creativity.

Monday
_____
_____
_____
_____
_____

Tuesday
_____
_____
_____
_____
_____

Wednesday
_____
_____
_____
_____
_____

Thursday

Friday

Saturday

Sunday

WEEK 23

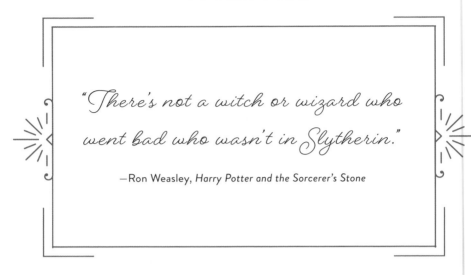

"There's not a witch or wizard who went bad who wasn't in Slytherin."

—Ron Weasley, *Harry Potter and the Sorcerer's Stone*

The above quote, spoken by Ron Weasley during the Sorting Ceremony in *Harry Potter and the Sorcerer's Stone*, illustrates the fact that stereotypes exist even in the wizarding world. Whether it's the belief that all Slytherins are "bad" or that all Ravenclaws are "eccentric," these stereotypes can be hurtful and unfair. What are some general stereotypes about Ravenclaws that you feel are unfair? What do you say when confronted by them?

WEEK 24

RAVENCLAW MOMENTS:

Daily Acts of Wisdom, Wit, and Creativity

Monday

_____

_____

_____

_____

_____

Tuesday

_____

_____

_____

_____

_____

Wednesday

_____

_____

_____

_____

_____

Thursday

Friday

Saturday

Sunday

WEEK 24

"But, listen, if it really means that much to you, you can choose . . . The Sorting Hat takes your choice into account."

—Harry Potter, *Harry Potter and the Deathly Hallows – Part 2*

In the Harry Potter films, the Sorting Hat was originally planning to put Harry in Slytherin, but he pleaded with the hat not to, and the Sorting Hat accepted his choice. Given the choice, would you choose to be in Ravenclaw? Why or why not?

WEEK 25

RAVENCLAW MOMENTS:

Daily Acts of Wisdom, Wit, and Creativity

Monday

Tuesday

Wednesday

Thursday

Friday

Saturday

Sunday

WEEK 25

IN *HARRY POTTER AND THE SORCERER'S STONE*, Harry, Ron, Hermione, and Draco Malfoy are caught out of bed at night and sentenced to detention in the Forbidden Forest. Imagine you've been sentenced to detention at Hogwarts. Based on your personality as a Ravenclaw, what rules do you think you'd be most likely to break and why?

WEEK 26

RAVENCLAW MOMENTS:
Daily Acts of Wisdom, Wit, and Creativity

Monday

Tuesday

Wednesday

Thursday

Friday

Saturday

Sunday

WEEK 26

IN *HARRY POTTER AND THE PRISONER OF AZKABAN,*
Professor Lupin teaches the third-year students how to repel a Boggart,
a Dark creature that takes the form of whatever the person fears the most.
Do you have any specific fears that relate to your identity as a Ravenclaw?
Fear of failure? Fear of being second best? Write these down below.
On the following page where it says "Riddikulus!" write what you would use
to repel the Boggart if it turned into what you fear.

ABOVE: The Boggart version of Potions Master Severus Snape, dressed as Neville Longbottom's
grandmother. Design by Jany Temime, drawn by Laurent Guinci.

Riddikulus!

ABOVE: Concept art of the jack-in-the-box version of the Boggart by Rob Bliss.

WEEK 27

RAVENCLAW MOMENTS:
Daily Acts of Wisdom, Wit, and Creativity

Monday

Tuesday

Wednesday

Thursday

Friday

Saturday

Sunday

WEEK 27

THINK ABOUT THE HOUSE that you find the most difficult to relate to. What is it about that house that you, as a Ravenclaw, find difficult to understand or appreciate?

WEEK 28

RAVENCLAW MOMENTS:
Daily Acts of Wisdom, Wit, and Creativity

Monday

Tuesday

Wednesday

Thursday

Friday

Saturday

Sunday

WEEK 28

WHILE WE NEVER SEE THE RAVENCLAW COMMON ROOM
in the films, we can imagine what it would look like based on the
personality of the house. Look around your own living space. What items
or elements do you feel reflect your tastes as a Ravenclaw?

WEEK 29

RAVENCLAW MOMENTS:
Daily Acts of Wisdom, Wit, and Creativity

Monday

Tuesday

Wednesday

Thursday

Friday

Saturday

Sunday

WEEK 29

THE HARRY POTTER FILMS ARE FILLED with examples of romantic pairings between people from different houses, such as Lupin and Tonks, Harry and Cho, and Neville and Luna. Consider your ideal romantic partner. Are they in the same house as you? What house do they belong to and why?

WEEK 30

Monday

_____

_____

_____

_____

Tuesday

_____

_____

_____

_____

Wednesday

_____

_____

_____

_____

Thursday

Friday

Saturday

Sunday

WEEK 30

IMAGINE YOUR HOUSE JUST WON the House Cup.
How would you celebrate? Use this space to jot down some ideas
for the perfect House Cup party that Ravenclaws everywhere
would love to attend.

WEEK 31

RAVENCLAW MOMENTS:

Daily Acts of Wisdom, Wit, and Creativity

Monday

Tuesday

Wednesday

Thursday

Friday

Saturday

Sunday

WEEK 31

WHEN FIRST-YEAR HOGWARTS STUDENTS are sorted into their houses, they are only eleven years old. Do you think you would have been sorted into Ravenclaw when you were eleven? How have you changed or grown since then?

WEEK 32

RAVENCLAW MOMENTS:
Daily Acts of Wisdom, Wit, and Creativity

Monday

Tuesday

Wednesday

Thursday

Friday

Saturday

Sunday

WEEK 32

IN *HARRY POTTER AND THE HALF-BLOOD PRINCE*,
Harry is given the task of retrieving a memory from Professor Slughorn.
This poses a bit of a problem as the reluctant professor does his best to
avoid Harry once he realizes what Harry's trying to do. Harry eventually
solves the problem by taking a dose of Felix Felicis and appealing to
Slughorn's memory of Harry's mother. As a Ravenclaw, how do you solve
problems? When was the last time you used your Ravenclaw qualities to
solve a problem and how?

WEEK 33

RAVENCLAW MOMENTS:

Daily Acts of Wisdom, Wit, and Creativity

Monday

Tuesday

Wednesday

Thursday

Friday

Saturday

Sunday

WEEK 33

IN *HARRY POTTER AND THE ORDER OF THE PHOENIX,*
Harry mistakenly believes a vision sent to him by Lord Voldemort
that shows his godfather, Sirius, in danger. Harry rushes to his
godfather's aid, an action that eventually leads to Sirius's death.
Think about the last time you made a mistake. Were there any aspects
of your identity as a Ravenclaw that played a part in the situation?
What could you have done differently?

WEEK 34

RAVENCLAW MOMENTS:

Daily Acts of Wisdom, Wit, and Creativity

Monday

Tuesday

Wednesday

Thursday

Friday

Saturday

Sunday

WEEK 34

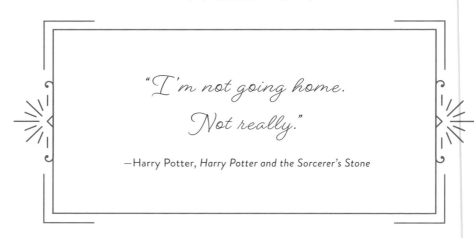

> *"I'm not going home.*
> *Not really."*
>
> —Harry Potter, *Harry Potter and the Sorcerer's Stone*

Everyone has special places in their lives.
Places where they feel the most like themselves. For Harry,
this is Hogwarts. Think about a space that is important to you
as a Ravenclaw. How does this space bring out those qualities
that symbolize your inner Ravenclaw?

WEEK 35

RAVENCLAW MOMENTS:

Daily Acts of Wisdom, Wit, and Creativity

Monday

Tuesday

Wednesday

Thursday

Friday

Saturday

Sunday

WEEK 35

IN *HARRY POTTER AND THE GOBLET OF FIRE*, Harry faces a Hungarian Horntail guarding a golden egg as the first task of the Triwizard Tournament. He uses his broomstick to complete the task, a decision that plays into his assets as a Gryffindor. How would you use your Ravenclaw qualities—wisdom and creativity—to achieve this task?

ABOVE: Concept art of Harry battling the Hungarian Horntail by Paul Catling.

ABOVE: More concept art of Harry and the Hungarian Horntail by Paul Catling.

WEEK 36

RAVENCLAW MOMENTS:

Daily Acts of Wisdom, Wit, and Creativity

Monday

Tuesday

Wednesday

Thursday

_____
_____
_____
_____
_____

Friday

_____
_____
_____
_____

Saturday

_____
_____
_____
_____

Sunday

_____
_____
_____
_____

WEEK 36

IN *HARRY POTTER AND THE CHAMBER OF SECRETS,*
Harry discovers he can speak Parseltongue, a skill that frightens him due
to its association with Dark wizards. Have you ever discovered something
about yourself that frightened you? How can you use your assets as a
Ravenclaw to overcome that fear?

WEEK 37

RAVENCLAW MOMENTS:

Daily Acts of Wisdom, Wit, and Creativity

Monday

Tuesday

Wednesday

Thursday

Friday

Saturday

Sunday

WEEK 37

WHILE LIFE IN THE HARRY POTTER FILMS never lacks excitement, in the real world, we all get bored from time to time. But boredom can be addressed with just a little creativity. Make a list of ten things you could do right now to challenge, interest, or inspire your inner Ravenclaw. Refer back to this the next time you need some inspiration.

1.

2.

3.

4.

5.

6.

7.

8.

9.

10.

WEEK 38

RAVENCLAW MOMENTS:
Daily Acts of Wisdom, Wit, and Creativity

Monday

Tuesday

Wednesday

Thursday

Friday

Saturday

Sunday

COLORING MEDITATIONS

Rowena Ravenclaw's diadem is an iconic Ravenclaw artifact. In the film, the diadem is shaped like a raven and features Rowena Ravenclaw's maxim, "Wit beyond measure is man's greatest treasure," inscribed along the bottom edge. What artifacts in your own life represent your identity as a Ravenclaw? Color in the diadem below, and then decorate the opposite page with illustrations, taped or glued-in ephemera, or other embellishments that symbolize these artifacts.

WEEK 39

RAVENCLAW MOMENTS:
Daily Acts of Wisdom, Wit, and Creativity

Monday

Tuesday

Wednesday

Thursday

Friday

Saturday

Sunday

WEEK 39

"For in dreams we enter a world that is entirely our own. Let them swim in the deepest ocean or glide over the highest cloud."

—Professor Dumbledore, *Harry Potter and the Prisoner of Azkaban*

Our dreams can reveal a lot about our inner world. Write down a recent dream you had and how it relates to your identity as a Ravenclaw.

_____

_____

_____

_____

_____

_____

_____

_____

WEEK 40

RAVENCLAW MOMENTS:

Daily Acts of Wisdom, Wit, and Creativity

Monday

Tuesday

Wednesday

Thursday

Friday

Saturday

Sunday

WEEK 40

IMAGINE YOU'VE BEEN MADE prefect at Hogwarts.
It's your job to help guide the new first-years in Ravenclaw.
Write down five pieces of advice you would give them to help
them embrace their Ravenclaw identity.

1.

2.

3.

4.

5.

WEEK 41

RAVENCLAW MOMENTS:
Daily Acts of Wisdom, Wit, and Creativity

Monday

Tuesday

Wednesday

Thursday

Friday

Saturday

Sunday

WEEK 41

IN THE HARRY POTTER FILMS, Harry encounters many adult figures who he looks up to and respects—people like Remus Lupin, Minerva McGonagall, and even Severus Snape—who help shape his development into a hero. Think about a real-word Ravenclaw in your life who has inspired you. What about this person do you most admire and respect?

WEEK 42

RAVENCLAW MOMENTS:

Daily Acts of Wisdom, Wit, and Creativity

Monday

Tuesday

Wednesday

Thursday

Friday

Saturday

Sunday

WEEK 42

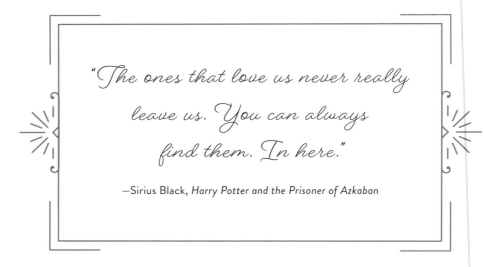

"The ones that love us never really leave us. You can always find them. In here."

—Sirius Black, *Harry Potter and the Prisoner of Azkaban*

Think about someone you've lost in your life, either through death or another circumstance. Reflect on your relationship with that person and what they taught you. Did they play any part in your development as a Ravenclaw? How so?

WEEK 43

RAVENCLAW MOMENTS:

Daily Acts of Wisdom, Wit, and Creativity

Monday

Tuesday

Wednesday

Thursday

Friday

Saturday

Sunday

THE WIZARDING WORLD IS FULL of an astonishing array of magical creatures: dragons, Hippogriffs, house-elves, centaurs, phoenixes, and more. What creature do you think embodies similar traits to those of Ravenclaw house? How can you bring the spirit of that creature into your daily life?

ABOVE LEFT: Concept art of a Thestral by Rob Bliss.
ABOVE RIGHT: Concept art of Fawkes the phoenix by Adam Brockbank.

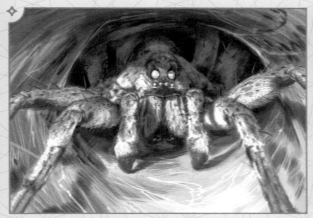

CLOCKWISE FROM TOP LEFT: Concept art of Aragog in his lair by Adam Brockbank; a centaur draws his bow, also by Adam Brockbank; Harry riding Buckbeak the Hippogriff, art by Dermot Power.

WEEK 44

Monday

Tuesday

Wednesday

Thursday

Friday

Saturday

Sunday

WEEK 44

IN THE HARRY POTTER FILMS, there are moments of great danger and grief, especially in the later films as the wizarding world becomes enveloped in a devastating war against Lord Voldemort. In the real world, everyone deals with stress, pain, and emotional upheaval from time to time. That's why it's important to prioritize self-care. As a Ravenclaw, what does self-care mean to you? How do you take care of yourself when faced with stress or pain?

WEEK 45

RAVENCLAW MOMENTS:

Daily Acts of Wisdom, Wit, and Creativity

Monday

Tuesday

Wednesday

Thursday

Friday

Saturday

Sunday

WEEK 45

YOU'VE JUST LANDED A MAJOR JOB INTERVIEW.

How can you use your assets as a Ravenclaw to get the job?

Make a list of five things you can do to prepare.

1. _____

_____

_____

_____

_____

_____

_____

2. _____

_____

_____

_____

_____

_____

3. _____

4. _____

5. _____

WEEK 46

RAVENCLAW MOMENTS:
Daily Acts of Wisdom, Wit, and Creativity

Monday

Tuesday

Wednesday

Thursday

Friday

Saturday

Sunday

WEEK 46

THERE ARE SEVERAL GREAT EXAMPLES of Ravenclaw heroes in the Harry Potter films: Luna Lovegood, Cho Chang, and not to mention all the Ravenclaws that joined Dumbledore's Army. What do you think defines a Ravenclaw hero? How can you, as a Ravenclaw, be a hero to someone in your life?

WEEK 47

RAVENCLAW MOMENTS:

Daily Acts of Wisdom, Wit, and Creativity

Monday

_____

_____

_____

_____

Tuesday

_____

_____

_____

_____

Wednesday

_____

_____

_____

_____

Thursday

Friday

Saturday

Sunday

WEEK 47

IN *HARRY POTTER AND THE CHAMBER OF SECRETS,*
Draco Malfoy goads Ron Weasley into attacking him by calling Hermione a
foul name, an act that plays into Ron's Gryffindor qualities of chivalry and
determination. Has anybody ever used your traits as a Ravenclaw against you?
What could you have done differently?

WEEK 48

RAVENCLAW MOMENTS:
Daily Acts of Wisdom, Wit, and Creativity

Monday

Tuesday

Wednesday

Thursday

_____

_____

_____

_____

_____

Friday

_____

_____

_____

_____

_____

Saturday

_____

_____

_____

_____

_____

Sunday

_____

_____

_____

_____

_____

WEEK 48

IN *HARRY POTTER AND THE ORDER OF THE PHOENIX*, Harry and his friends start Dumbledore's Army, a secret student group dedicated to fighting Dolores Umbridge's rules and learning practical Defense Against the Dark skills. As a Ravenclaw, how can you stand up for what you believe in? What kind of steps do you feel you can take to contribute?

WEEK 49

RAVENCLAW MOMENTS:
Daily Acts of Wisdom, Wit, and Creativity

Monday

Tuesday

Wednesday

Thursday

Friday

Saturday

Sunday

WEEK 49

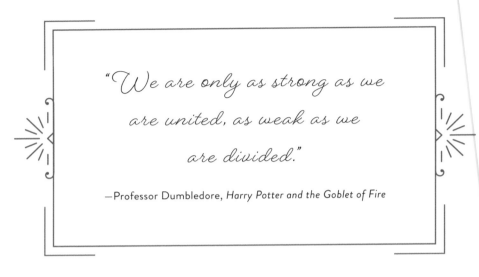

"We are only as strong as we
are united, as weak as we
are divided."

—Professor Dumbledore, *Harry Potter and the Goblet of Fire*

Think of a time you were in conflict with someone who
embodies the characteristics of another house. How were you
able to resolve the situation? Did your qualities as a Ravenclaw
prove to be an asset or an obstacle?

_____

_____

_____

_____

_____

_____

_____

WEEK 50

RAVENCLAW MOMENTS:

Daily Acts of Wisdom, Wit, and Creativity

Monday

Tuesday

Wednesday

Thursday

Friday

Saturday

Sunday

WEEK 50

AS EVERYONE KNOWS, the traits of Ravenclaw are wisdom, wit, and creativity. After fifty weeks of reflection and cultivation, which of these traits do you identify with the most? Which do you identify with the least? Are there any additional traits that you feel match the Ravenclaw profile that are not talked about as much?

WEEK 51

RAVENCLAW MOMENTS:

Daily Acts of Wisdom, Wit, and Creativity

Monday

Tuesday

Wednesday

Thursday

_____
_____
_____
_____
_____

Friday

_____
_____
_____
_____
_____

Saturday

_____
_____
_____
_____
_____

Sunday

_____
_____
_____
_____
_____

WEEK 51

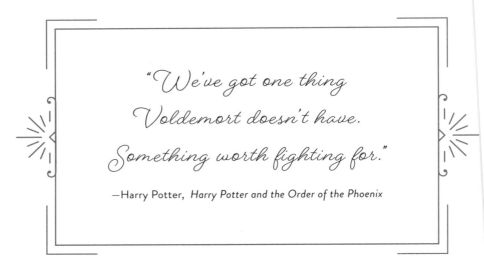

> "We've got one thing
> Voldemort doesn't have.
> Something worth fighting for."
>
> —Harry Potter, *Harry Potter and the Order of the Phoenix*

Everybody believes in fighting for something.
As a Ravenclaw, what do you think is worth fighting for?
How do you fight for it?

_____

_____

_____

_____

_____

_____

_____

WEEK 52

Monday

Tuesday

Wednesday

Thursday

Friday

Saturday

Sunday

WEEK 52

> *"Soon we must all face the choice between what is right and what is easy."*
>
> —Professor Dumbledore, *Harry Potter and the Goblet of Fire*

For this final prompt, reflect on what you've learned.
How do your qualities as a Ravenclaw help you make the right choices?

_____

_____

_____

_____

_____

_____

_____

_____

INSIGHT
EDITIONS

PO Box 3088
San Rafael, CA 94912
www.insighteditions.com

 Find us on Facebook: www.facebook.com/InsightEditions
Follow us on Twitter: @insighteditions

Library of Congress Cataloging-in-Publication Data available.

ISBN: 978-1-64722-238-3

Publisher: Raoul Goff
Associate Publisher: Vanessa Lopez
Creative Director: Chrissy Kwasnik
VP of Manufacturing: Alix Nicholaeff
Senior Designer: Ashley Quackenbush
Editor: Hilary VandenBroek
Editorial Assistant: Anna Wostenberg
Managing Editor: Lauren LaPera
Production Editor: Jennifer Bentham
Production Manager: Andy Harper

Text by Hilary VandenBroek

ROOTS of PEACE   REPLANTED PAPER

Insight Editions, in association with Roots of Peace, will plant two trees for each tree used in the manufacturing of this book. Roots of Peace is an internationally renowned humanitarian organization dedicated to
eradicating land mines worldwide and converting war-torn lands into productive farms and wildlife habitats.
Roots of Peace will plant two million fruit and nut trees in Afghanistan and provide farmers there with the
skills and support necessary for sustainable land use.

Manufactured in China by Insight Editions

10 9 8 7 6 5 4 3 2 1